Dad's Cake

Crabtree Publishing Company

www.crabtreebooks.com

1-800-387-7650

PMB 16A, 350 Fifth Ave.
Suite 3308,
New York, NY

616 Welland Ave.
St. Catharines, ON
L2M 5V6

Published by Crabtree Publishing in 2010

Series Editor: Jackie Hamley
Editor: Reagan Miller
Series Advisor: Dr. Hilary Minns
Series Designer: Peter Scoulding
Editorial Director: Kathy Middleton

Text © Margaret Nash 2008
Illustration © Jane Cope 2008

First published in 2008
by Franklin Watts
(A division of Hachette
Children's Books)

The rights of the author and the illustrator
of this Work have been asserted.

Library and Archives Canada Cataloguing in Publication

Nash, Margaret, 1939-
    Dad's cake / Margaret Nash ; illustrated by
Jane Cope.

(Tadpoles)
ISBN 978-0-7787-3865-7 (bound).--
ISBN 978-0-7787-3896-1 (pbk.)

    1. Readers (Primary). 2. Readers--Cake.
3. Readers--Fathers and sons. I. Cope, Jane
II. Title. III. Series: Tadpoles (St. Catharines, Ont.)

PE1117.T33 2009   428.6   C2009-903983-4

Library of Congress Cataloging-in-Publication Data

Nash, Margaret, 1939-
 Dad's cake / by Margaret Nash ; illustrated by
Jane Cope.
     p. cm. -- (Tadpoles)
 Summary: Dad asks Jed to help him make a cake
with strange ingredients which keeps Jed guessing
as to who this cake is for.
 ISBN 978-0-7787-3896-1 (pbk. : alk. paper) -- ISBN
978-0-7787-3865-7 (reinforced lib. bdg. : alk. paper)
 [1. Fathers and sons--Fiction. 2. Baking--Fiction.
3. Cake--Fiction. 4. Humorous stories.] I. Cope,
Jane, ill. II. Title. III. Series.

PZ7.N1732Dc 2009
 [E]--dc22
                                            2009025291

Dad's Cake

by Margaret Nash

Illustrated by Jane Cope

Crabtree Publishing Company

www.crabtreebooks.com

Margaret Nash

"Cakes are yummy! My son once made one in a very small tin. When it came out of the oven it was almost as tall as a chimney!"

Jane Cope

"I love making cakes, although eating them is the best bit! Unless it's a cake like the one Dad is making ..."

"Let's make a cake,"
said Dad.

"Who for?" said Jed.

"Ah!" said Dad.

"You will see!"

Dad gave Jed a
bowl and a very
big spoon, then ...

9

... a bit of this,

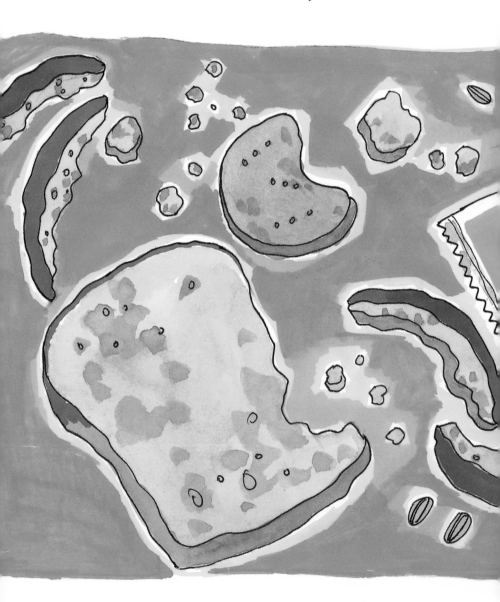

and a lot of these ...

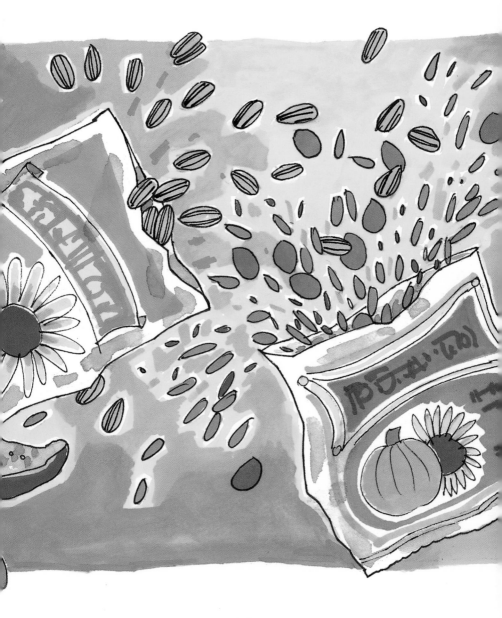

... scraps of fat,

and lumps of cheese.

"Yuck!" said Jed.
"Who will want
this cake?"

"Not me!" said Dad.
"But someone will!"

"But Dad, **nobody** will want this cake!" said Jed.

"Ah!" said Dad.
"They will! You will
see!"

21

And they did!

Notes for adults

TADPOLES are structured to provide support for early readers. The stories may also be used by adults for sharing with young children.

Starting to read alone can be daunting. **TADPOLES** help by providing visual support and repeating high frequency words and phrases. These books will both develop confidence and encourage reading and rereading for pleasure.

If you are reading this book with a child, here are a few suggestions:

1. Make reading fun! Choose a time to read when you and the child are relaxed and have time to share the story.
2. Talk about the story before you start reading. Look at the cover and the blurb. What might the story be about? Why might the child like it?
3. Encourage the child to reread the story, and to retell the story in their own words, using the illustrations to remind them what has happened.
4. Discuss the story and see if the child can relate it to their own experiences, or perhaps compare it to another story they know.
5. Give praise! Children learn best in a positive environment.

If you enjoyed this book, why not try another TADPOLES story?

At the End of the Garden
9780778738503 RLB
9780778738817 PB

Bad Luck, Lucy!
9780778738510 RLB
9780778738824 PB

Ben and the Big Balloon
9780778738602 RLB
9780778738916 PB

Crabby Gabby
9780778738527 RLB
9780778738831 PB

Dad's Cake
9780778738657 RLB
9780778738961 PB

Dad's Van
9780778738664 RLB
9780778738978 PB

The Dinosaur Next Door
9780778738732 RLB
9780778739043 PB

Five Teddy Bears
9780778738534 RLB
9780778738848 PB

I'm Taller Than You!
9780778738541 RLB
9780778738855 PB

Leo's New Pet
9780778738558 RLB
9780778738862 PB

Little Troll
9780778738565 RLB
9780778738879 PB

Mop Top
9780778738572 RLB
9780778738886 PB

My Auntie Susan
9780778738589 RLB
9780778738893 PB

My Big, New Bed
9780778738596 RLB
9780778738909 PB

Night, Night
9780778738671 RLB
9780778738985 PB

Over the Moon!
9780778738688 RLB
9780778738992 PB

Pirate Pete
9780778738619 RLB
9780778738923 PB

Rooster's Alarm
9780778738749 RLB
9780778739050 PB

Runny Honey
9780778738626 RLB
9780778738930 PB

The Sad Princess
9780778738725 RLB
9780778739036 PB

Sammy's Secret
9780778738633 RLB
9780778738947 PB

Sam's Sunflower
9780778738640 RLB
9780778738954 PB

Tag!
9780778738695 RLB
9780778739005 PB

Ted's Party Bus
9780778738701 RLB
9780778739012 PB

Tortoise Races Home
9780778738718 RLB
9780778739029 PB